THE MAN WHO KEPT HOUSE

The Man

Who Kept House

RETOLD BY
Kathleen and Michael Hague

ILLUSTRATED BY
Michael Hague

HARCOURT BRACE JOVANOVICH   NEW YORK AND LONDON

Printed in the United States of America

Library of Congress Cataloging in Publication Data
Hague, Kathleen.
The man who kept house.

Summary: Convinced his work in the fields is
harder than his wife's work at home,
a farmer trades places with her for the day.
[1. Folklore—Norway]
I. Hague, Michael, joint author.   II. Title.
PZ8.1.H123Man   398.2'2'09481 [E]   80-26258
ISBN 0-15-251698-0   ISBN 0-15-251699-9 (pbk.)

B C D E   FIRST EDITION   B C D E (pbk.)

Were there ever any who worked as hard and long as the women of the house? Perhaps. Perhaps not. This is the story of one peevish man who was convinced that his wife had too little to do.

He came home daily from the fields, telling anyone who would listen how hard he had toiled while his wife only puttered about the house all day, breaking her leisure just long enough to fix his humble supper.

One particular evening he arrived home in a very foul mood, scornful because his supper was not yet on the table.

"Were I to spend the whole of my day," said the man, "doing nothing more than a few meager chores, I could surely have a hot meal ready for my hard-working husband."

"Oh, don't go on so," said the woman, placing his supper before him. "If you like, we'll change jobs tomorrow. I'll mow hay in the fields, and you can do the housework."

The man laughed out loud and said that he liked the idea. The experience would teach his wife what work was, he said.

Before dawn the wife arose and made ready for her day in the fields. She tied her hair back, packed a lunch, shouldered her husband's scythe, and set out. The man also rose early and went about the house, reading his carefully written list of chores.

"If only women could be
this organized," he said,
"what a better place
the world would be."

He sang as he washed the morning
dishes, until one of the plates slipped
from his hand and broke on the floor
with a crash. This woke the baby,
who made an even louder noise,
demanding something to eat.
Leaving the dirty dishes, the man
got breakfast ready for the child.

After a few mouthfuls had been
gobbled up, the baby began to flip
the oatmeal skyward with his spoon.
In graceful arcs it flew and landed
splat, splat, splat on the ceiling.

"Thank you. Thank you very much," shouted the man to the child. "Now are you happy? Look at the mess you have made for me. You would never do this if your mother were home!"

He took the bowl and put it in the sink. Then he wiped away the oatmeal, except for those lumps highest on the ceiling.

"My wife won't notice that," he said to himself, "and I'll bury the broken dish in the yard."

Now the man went into the bedroom to make up the beds.

"Just watch me," he said to the child, who was sitting on the foot of the bed, "and I'll show you how skillfully beds can be made. First I smooth the sheets and the blankets, and then I plump up the pillows." The baby clapped approvingly.

"Why, thank you!" said the smiling man, picking up the child. Quickly his smile disappeared when he found that the baby had soiled the bed. With a sigh he changed its diapers.

Then he took the sheets off the bed and carried the dirty laundry out to wash in a tub in the yard. He scrubbed the sheets and diapers vigorously. When they were clean, he rinsed and shook them out and began to hang them on the line to dry. Suddenly the sound of squealing and laughter filled his ears. The baby and the pig had tumbled into the tub!

"Oh, no!" shouted the man as he rushed to save them both from drowning.

Meanwhile, the sheets flapped in the breeze, slid to the ground, and danced with the wind in the mud. Grimly the man retrieved them and took them back for another round of scrubbing. This time, he tethered the baby to a tree and put the pig in its pen. Soon, the sheets were white again and hung gaily on the line, secured with twenty clothespins.

It was long past lunchtime now, and inside the house the
man and child shared a meal of bread, cheese, and milk. Then
the man rocked the child to sleep and gently laid him in the
kitchen cradle to nap.

"At last," said the man to himself, "I will get some work
done."

He washed the dirty dishes, then remembered he would have
to churn some butter for dinner. He got out the churn and put
in the cream, and after churning a while he felt quite thirsty.

"There would be no harm in sipping a bit of ale," he said.

He was in the cellar, tapping the ale, when he heard a great commotion above.

"Now what!" he howled.

He rushed up the stairs and found the room in chaos.

Bowls and spoons, table and chairs were flying through the air as the goat ran bleating from one end of the room to the other, trying to find its way outside again. He dispatched the goat and stared in disbelief at the room. The churn was overturned and its contents were being noisily consumed by the pig, who had escaped his pen and entered with the goat. The baby had awakened and found pulling the tail of the cat most amusing, and the cat in trying to escape through the window knocked the newly washed dishes to the floor.

Panicked by the shouts from his master and the crash of the falling dishes, the pig turned and ran head-first into the wall, never to stir again. The man stared at the tap still in his hand and rushed down the stairs to find the cellar floor awash with ale and the barrel completely dry.

In a daze he climbed the stairs again. Opening the kitchen door, he gasped, "My wife! She'll be home any minute!"

Frantically he picked up the broken dishes, set up the table, chairs, and churn, and mopped up the floor. Taking no chances on further disaster, he tied the baby in his chair. Carrying out the unfortunate pig, he remembered that the cow had spent the day in the barn with nothing to eat.

Since it was too late to take her to the pasture, he put her to graze on the roof, for they had a turf roof of thick green grass. Then it crossed his mind that the cow might fall off, so he looped one end of a rope around her head and slipped the other end down the chimney.

Back inside he tied the other end of the rope around his leg. "Do you see how clever your father is?" boasted the man to the baby while hanging a pot of water over the hearth to boil for soup. "Now if the cow moves too far, I can feel her tug at the rope on my leg. Your mother would never think of such a thing!"

Just then the cow did fall off the roof.

But instead of a gentle tug, there was a tremendous yank, and the man was pulled halfway up the chimney, his head hanging inches above the pot of water.

"Help, help, help!" he shouted frantically. The man struggled but to no avail. The baby applauded his father's acrobatics, and the cow moaned.

The wife, having worked in the fields all day, admitted that it was indeed hard work and started for home. Catching sight of the house from a distance, she thought it strange to see no lights coming from the windows, so she quickened her pace.

Arriving at the house, her mouth fell open when she saw the unhappy cow dangling from the roof.

"What calamity is this?" she cried as she cut it down with the scythe.

A great splash came from within, and she rushed inside to find the baby tied to his chair and, in the hearth, her husband with his head in the pot.

The wife asked no questions and the husband made no comments about the day's events. But, from that day on, nothing but praise ever passed the man's lips in speaking of his wife, and his courtesy to the women of the town was noticed by all.